Aliens

Tessa Krailing

Tessa and Tony went into the joke shop.
'We want a joke,' said Tony.
'Do you have a good one?' asked Tessa.

'How about masks?' said Mr Miller, as he picked two out of the box.
'They will make you look like aliens.
Put the masks on and people will think you have come from another planet.'

The twins were pleased with the masks.
They gave Mr Miller some money and
left the shop.
'Let's go into the park,' said Tony.
'We can play a joke on Fred.'

red was cleaning the windows of his shed.
essa and Tony put the masks on and
umped out at him.
We are aliens!' they shouted.
We have come to take over this planet and
lean it up.'

'That's good,' said Fred.
'You can clean up this park first.
People are always dropping litter.
You can clean that up!'

'Fred didn't think we were aliens,'
said Tessa.
'Let's pick up the litter,' said Tony.
'It will give us something to do.
There is a lot under this bench.'

THE
DUKE
OF
WELLINGTON

7

Tessa found a letter under the bench.
'Here is a letter,' she said.
'Someone must have dropped it.
It is for Mrs Nash.
That's the old lady who lives at number 23.'

'I don't want to go in there,' said Tony.
'People say the old lady is mad!'
'We must give her the letter,' said Tessa.
'It might be important.'

'We could just put it through
the letter-box,' said Tony.
'Look,' said Tessa. 'She is opening
the door!'

10

Mrs Nash opened the door.
She saw the twins.
They gave her a terrible fright.

'Go away!' the old lady shouted.
'Go away, you monsters!
Don't come here again!'

12

'We frightened her,' said Tessa.
'It must have been the masks.
She thought we were aliens!'

'There she is,' said Tony.
'She is looking out of the window.'

The twins went up to the window.
'Look,' called the twins.
'We are not aliens.'
But Mrs Nash was too afraid to look.
She quickly shut the curtains.

A policeman was going by.
It was PC Kent.
'Now what's all this?' he asked.
'What are you kids doing in that garden?
Are you frightening poor old Mrs Nash?'

17

'We didn't want to frighten her,' said Tessa.
'We found this letter.
We only wanted to give it to her.
We thought it might be important but
she thought we were aliens!'

'Come with me,' said PC Kent.
'We must sort this out.
If we don't, she will be too frightened
to leave the house!'

'Mrs Nash,' called PC Kent.
'It is the police. Open the door.
You will be quite safe.'

Mrs Nash opened the curtains.
She saw PC Kent and opened
the door a little.
'Have they gone?' the old lady asked.
'Have those monsters gone?'

'They are not monsters,' said PC Kent.
'Look, they are just kids.
They came to give you a letter.
They found it in the park where
someone dropped it.
They thought it might be important.'

'I must have dropped it,' said Mrs Nash.
'Come inside.'
The twins didn't want to go inside.
They were afraid Mrs Nash was mad.

'I thought you were monsters,'
said the old lady.
'You gave me a terrible fright in
those masks.'
The twins didn't tell her that
they had been frightened too!